How I Became a Real Pirate...

by

Truly Owen Free

Copyright 2018 Truly O. Free

Treasure Hunt!

Welcome to my world y'all. Hope you found the place alright. Go ahead and have a seat if that makes you comfortable. Or you can read this thing standing up if you want. That works too. I may even come up with a water-proof edition later on. For reasons which should soon become obvious.

This book contains clues to an actual Hidden Pirate Treasure you can find, but only if you can figure out the Picture Puzzle Code. You'll have to read all three books to solve the whole thing. This one you're reading now, plus: <u>A Month in South America</u> and <u>Thirteen Fathoms and a Dead Man's Sweater</u>.

You can maybe glean more clues and hints from the other books I wrote too, if you're really into reading or something. Since they will let you know more about me, and where I've lived and adventured to. The unabridged version of this one alone will give you a much deeper view of everything, since I sure didn't become a dirty old pirate in just these few short pages. You know darn well that's not how real life works.

Reading that much nastier version may give you a better clue about what's in my Treasure Chest too, since I'm not gonna show *everything* on the interweb. There has to be some kinda surprise at the end.

I did this for you, because I love hunting treasure too, and I have gotten really lucky a few times. So I wanted to share that one of a kind experience with others. That feeling of finding something uniquely mystic, and cast away in time. I also wanted to create something awesome to light up a few lives if I could. Since I gotta pay down all this Bad Old Pirate Karma somehow.

But I hope you brought along your Voodoo pajamas too, because this book is also a magical gate. An entrance back to where we all really come from, and that place where all the lines are blurred. Between what you think is real and what actual dreams may be. A walk behind secret moonlight, a sail on the misty gloom sea, an island of sweet bright starshine, a door with a well hidden key.

Cross over with me now, back to the Primordial Woods, but take heed before we depart. You may not be the same when you return.

If you're scared about such things: Spirits, ghosts, death, the underworld, hard work, drowning. Then turn back now. I didn't really want you my finding my treasure anyway. I'm a *real* pirate. Whether I wanna be or not. Like I was born this way, or cursed. So this ain't gonna be easy for *you* either.

This is also a **Smart-Phone Interactive Story**™**,** so you can see pictures of the actual treasure I've hidden, right now, by following the

QR code below to my very exclusive but highly popular website empire.

(trulyowenfree.net).

There's a whole bunch of other cool stuff on there too, and there are more QR codes later in the book that will lead you to other secret rooms on the site. Which can only be accessed through this book.

I'd say it's a bit of a Treasure Race now too, because other people are out there searching, but that's just how *real* treasure hunting is. To the Victor goes the spoils. Of course, this particular treasure probably won't qualify you as spoiled, or even make you super rich by most people's standards. Though it is worth a considerable amount of money ($70,000+), which is definitely enough to get you started in another direction, or out of a financial hole.

So I hope that someone who really needs it is the winner.

And of course the treasure is made of actual gold and silver, and it has one of a kind jewelery in it, and sharp brutal weapons, and jingling spendable coins, and shiny beautiful gemstones. Just like any really awesome hidden treasure should. And there is definitely enough seriously cool stuff in the Treasure Chest to share with a family or team too. Or you can just keep it all for yourself, and be a stingy old Scrooge. Nobody will hold it against you. At least not me anyway.

I'm a pirate.

However too, after you read all these stories and do your homework, to discover who I actually am, you will surely realize that I am no joke, and that all of this is *really* real. And also that I have probably hidden something one-of-a-kind marvelous out there too. Like the anciently awesome shiny stuff you only see in movies. So whoever finds it first is gonna end up kinda famous, and start living a whole other new kind of life. Just like me...Truly Owen Free.

Shoot, even if you just go out searching for my treasure, you're gonna' go on the most amazing adventure most of you have ever had. I hid the treasure some place totally beautiful, but where most people in the United States can travel to on a fairly modest budget. I'm thinking $500.00 per person, or even less than that. If you're savvy.

So this one ain't just for the Rich Folks either, kids. Anyone can find this treasure, <u>if they are at least somewhat physically fit</u>, and it's not even that far from town. Even if it cost you all your cash to get there, you'll get it all back several times over, and have an amazing time doing it.

Pirate pinkie swear.

The directions are quite specific, if you have any kind of puzzle-brain in your head. So you won't find any vaguely dangerous poetry lurking around here my friends. The Treasure Map is right here in the stories, and the words will guide you home. Before it's all over I will <u>definitely</u> dig the chest up, and stick a few more goodies in there too. Since I find lost shiny stuff all the time, without even trying too hard.

I don't care much about keeping those kinda things anyway, or need the money. Since I'm also a professional salvage diver, a gourmet chef, a full-on carpenter, and I can climb any tree you point to with a chainsaw strapped to me. So don't you worry about me. In fact, since I like you so much already, here's a few Big Clues to get you started:

Clue #1. The Hidden Pirate Treasure of Truly Owen Free is buried in one of the places I lived in or traveled to, in the three stories. And it's <u>not</u> in far-off South America...which is where I live now...so don't be trying to come find me for some dumb interview either. I'm not as friendly as I sound on paper. Fair warning.

Big Clue #2. You have to read all three books to crack The Picture Puzzle Code, and remember: Not all puzzles have four sides, but good ones often have at least that many layers.

And the **Biggest Clue of all, #3**. Look for what seems Out of Place in the stories to find the other Clues and crack the code. Also, don't forget that language is culture, multiple cultures used the area where the treasure is hidden, and we all live in a very digital culture.

You're also gonna need some...

Standard-Issue Treasure Hunting Gear:

1.   A decent vehicle. Drive yours, rent one, or buy an old beater near the chest. Then shove it off a cliff or give it away once you're rich. You could probably do this all by bicycle or bus too, or even walk or hitch-hike really, but someone else will probably beat you there.

2.   A decent compass, and know how to read it.

3.   At least a cheap metal detector. I personally found way more treasure with an old used one I got for forty bucks, than I ever have with

my expensive one. But you can go all out if you want. A couple of the items *are* buried kinda deep. So gear yourself accordingly.

4.   Some time off from work or school. With pay, if you can.

5.   Some clear-tape and a pair of scissors.

6.   A shovel. Folding ones are best.

7.   A <u>good</u> piece of rope for safety, or for lowering things. Twenty five feet should be plenty for most folks, but <u>more</u> if you live where there are no hills, or aren't very agile. Don't forget that cheap ropes fail, and no treasure is worth your life or health. Skimp <u>not</u> on this one, and learn a couple good climbing knots *before* you go.

8.   Good hiking shoes, and a pair of leather gloves.

9.   Plenty of food and water, and a really good bag to carry all that stuff (and the treasure) in.

10. Bug spray <u>and</u> sunscreen...and let's pay extra close attention to the weather while you're out there too folks. Though I'm sure you already knew that.

Also, a note on how to read this story, since I don't write exactly within the bounds of what your reading teacher will tell you is correct and proper English. I type like I actually speak, a bit manic and all over the place, and in case you don't know anything, or have watched too many movies, real pirates don't talk with silly English accents.

Us down-south, Gulf Coast bad boys, the kind of pirates that you *really* have to watch out for, tend to talk with more of a country drawl, and take longer breaks between each sentence for effect. But then make up for it by taking less of a pause when there is only a comma and say our longer sentences in more of a soothing flowing stream. Therefore what appear to be only sentence fragments are really whole statements for your mind to paint the rest of the colors into, so if you read this thing too fast, it might come across choppy and not as enjoyable. Slow down a little. Breathe. And let it all have time to sink in.

If you really want the full effect, try reading it in your best New Orleans Creole accent, with an extra helping of Florida Swamp Redneck thrown in there for authenticity. And don't forget to color the pictures in all your favorite colors. Magic markers sold seperately.

Oh and finally, this story <u>is</u> a complete and total made-up work of fiction. Any characters or scenarios that seem to be based in reality, are all just some sort of Occidental accident, or at least a very strange coincidence anyway. The whole following narrative is really just another scraped together tall tale, puked out onto the unsuspecting world by a lonely old boat scrubber from lower Oklahoma. All just to try and get out of debt for that (mostly) useless college education I got.

What a scam, right?

Kinda makes you wonder who the pirates really are.

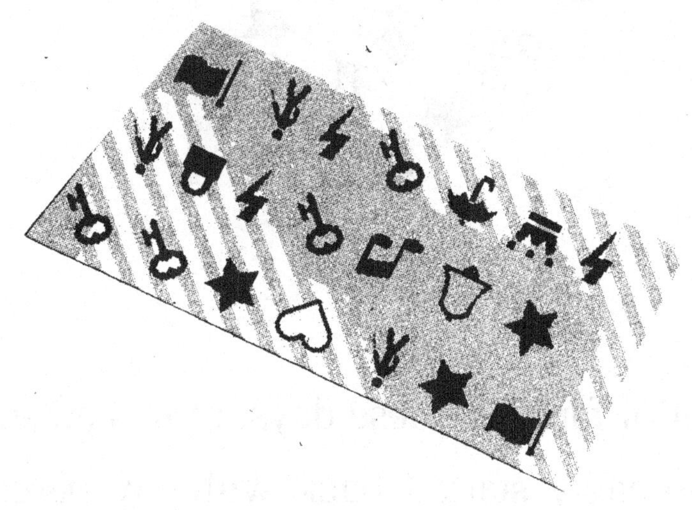

This book is for anyone who has ever been lost. Home is wherever you are. If you can find it.

Chapter 1 – The Blue Lady

Like a whole lot of families these days, mine had some really serious problems. It all probably started back with my parent's parents' great grandparents' parents or something, so nobody will ever figure out whose fault it all was. It doesn't even matter really. All I know is my mom and dad decided not to stay together anymore. Just like some of your folks, I'm sure.

After that, my mom and I moved a hundred miles away to some new little town. Surely to get away from the memories and the pain, or maybe she just found a better job there or something. I don't know. I was only like four years old. What could I know?

I didn't really understand much of anything that was going on back then. Only that things were very different all of a sudden, and that we lived somewhere else new and strange now. Though I'm sure I was pretty much alright with all that stuff. As long as I got to keep playing outside, and meals were prepared on time.

Shoot, to tell you the truth, I don't remember being all that upset at all about Dear Old Dad not being around anymore, because my mom got us a mixed-breed mutt-dog from the pound. Who I named Sandy. Because of her shaggy dirty-blond coat.

That dog was so loyal, that she used to get *between* me and my mom whenever I was about to get a spanking. So I'm sure you can imagine how upset I was when Sandy didn't get to go on a certain Road Trip with us (my very first one). Back to our old town. To visit one of my mother's old friends for the weekend.

No seriously, I really loved that dog, and she doesn't even have anything else to do with the story either. I just wanted to write about her, because I promised. There you go sweet doggy. I *told* you I would bring you back to life if I could. Now we can both live forever.

Here inside this book.

We made the trip at night after my mother finished her shift at the hospital. I fell asleep on the way to the hum of the road passing beneath our wheels. She might have even sung me to sleep or something, because good mothers tend to do stuff like that, or at least mine sure did.

"Truly...we're here." she said in her sweet sing-song voice.

It seemed like I just dozed off on the outskirts of our new town, but then...BLINK!...we had already arrived in the old one. Like instantly or something. And I remember feeling really strange about it at the time, because it was the first time anything like that happened to me, so I thought maybe it was Magic® or something. Now I know it's just what happens when you're really tired, or you go for a long enough car ride.

BLINK!

Our car headlights cast long stripes of light deep into the shadowy pines as we turned left into her friend's driveway. Then came to a stop in front of her plain brown country house. We left most of our stuff in the car because it was really late. I stumbled and mumbled all puffy-eyed into the house, like sleepy little kids often do, then fell right back to sleep wherever mom put me.

Between then and dawn I had a wonderful dream.

I dreamed I got up from where I was sleeping and went back outside to look in the car, for a toy or something, but it was locked and I couldn't get in. I knew I wasn't supposed to wake anybody, or I would get in trouble, but that really didn't matter as much as the chance to be alone and outside (gulp) in the Deep Dark Woods at night. Which had also never happened to me before. Not back in the waking world anyway. We lived in town. So any punishments that might have come my way were surely worth the thrill.

Truth is, there's kinda nothing I like better than being totally scared out of my mind, and then dealing with it. Or traveling alone, and really far away from home. Where no one knows me, or could ever find me easily. And apparently I came out like that too.

A bit edgy, see?

A cool dreamy fresh-smelling mist was falling steadily, and I could hear it dripping off the trees all around me, but the warm glow of the yellow porch light only let me see across the road. Just to the edge of the Dark Shadowy Forest. Nothing else beyond that, except the deep dripping darkness. Then suddenly, I saw a tiny blue light. Way off back in the woods across the street. It grew and bounced along as it moved towards me. Illuminating the shadowy stands of trees and clearings as it passed. Like someone carrying a very small but very bright blue lantern. I crossed the road towards it, out of curiosity, and because for some reason I also wasn't scared anymore.

The little blue light continued to grow and move towards me, then quickened its pace so it met me at the other edge of the road. I must have turned back to the house, to make sure no one was waking up. Because in the second that I turned, then looked back again, the light became a tall and elegantly dressed Blue Lady, holding out her pale illuminated hand to me.

I took her long cool fingers in silence and followed her down the incline away from the road, then further a good distance through the wet leaves at our feet, until we joined an old trail leading even deeper into the Dark Misty Forest. Soon the trees we were passing became much larger and spaced further apart, so I knew we were in the older (and spookier) part of The Ancient Forest, and that there were *definitely* other creatures all around us. Hiding just out of sight in the darkness.

I knew I was safe with my lovely blue guide though, and I know she was speaking to me as we walked, because I remember the comforting tone of her voice. Like the sound of a fresh spring wind blowing through the trees, as it cools the sweat on your forehead. There were probably some wind-chimes and bird-songs thrown in there too. Because she was obviously a highly magical spirit, and they always talk like that, right?

Unfortunately, I don't remember much of what The Blue Lady was telling me that night, especially since this all happened a really long time ago. But I think she said something like, "Don't forget Truly, the crossed tools are number twenty four." Which I guess sounds really out of place, and kinda weird now that I think about it, but you know how freaky *those* kind of dreams can get. And you never know when they might lend a clue to some future event (wink).

Anyway, after a bit more walking we veered off and away from the trail, then climbed up and along a tall ridge, and eventually came down between the shadowy trees to a low darker hidden place. Where the fallen leaves were very deep and smelled like wet musty crawling things. She led me to an overhanging bit of earth, beneath the roots of a giant ancient tree. With Will-o-the-Wisp fireflies playing in its branches, or perched and glowing on its big dripping leaves. Pausing there, she knelt down next to me, reminded me to be silent with a long blue finger held tight to her lips, and pulled back a tangle of roots and leaves along the ground. To reveal a wondrously shining Hidden Treasure!

I can't recall exactly *what* the shiny treasure was that she showed me either. Only that it was very special, way shiny, and there was only one like it in the whole entire world. I also remember knowing that I was the only person in the world who knew about her, and what she knew, and how she lived out there alone in the oldest part of The Secret Forest.

You know how it is in dreams: You just Know stuff.

I woke up before everyone else, around daybreak, and I know I ran outside to look for The Blue Lady, because the dream had been *so* intensely life-like. Now in the daylight I could see that the forest across the street had a barbed-wire fence running along its border. There were houses and barns and livestock strewn all through the well-maintained woods and grounds now too. While back in the dream, there was only deep spooky dripping forest.

I remember that whole day knowing something really special had happened to me, and my life was gonna be different now. Like I had been picked for something good.

I kept hoping I would get to see The Blue Lady again too, and escape with her to that secret place she had taken me to. But I never did get the chance to explore those woods though, the ones *behind* the farm, because that weekend I had to go visit with my 'father', and do some other adult-important stuff with my mom and her friend. Then before I ever got a free hour to sneak away, we were on our way back to our new town, to live out our new lives, with a whole bunch of new people.

And for some other reason, we also never went back to that plain brown country house again. But that's just how it is these days, right?

Nobody stays together.

I thought about the dream and The Blue Lady from time to time, until I grew up. A couple times after that too. Especially if I was out in the woods alone, or riding in a car along a forest road at night. Because the whole experience was very *very* real to me. I had not had any other dreams like it up to then, and only a couple dreams as powerfully moving since. I know I gazed out the car window as we drove 'home' that weekend too, and wondered if The Blue Lady was out there. Somewhere all alone in the Spooky Ancient Forest.

Would she be alright? Was she lonely? Where did she sleep at night? What on Earth did she eat for dinner? Did she have a dog? And most importantly, where was that musty old ditch she took me to?

The one with the Treasure in it...

Chapter 3 – Treasure Hounds

After two solid weeks of chomping at the mouthpiece, and thinking I was gonna be stuck in boring old Tarpon City all summer, the Captain finally called to say a temporary position had opened up. On board his company's treasure salvage boat! They lost one diver to some family health problems, and their other one was on vacation. So if I could get myself down to the Florida Keys the very next day, I could be a paid treasure diver! Aboard a salvage vessel named the *Green Sea Daisy*.

I can't even begin to tell you how I felt. I could hardly believe it. I met Captain Borders a few months before, in the Dale Marlin treasure museum. Over there in Jupiter, Florida. And so far I had been doing a pretty good job of not letting myself get too excited. Even though the interview went really well. I promised myself I wouldn't get my hopes up, not until I actually set foot on the boat, but now...

Getting paid to dive?

For treasure?!

Down in the Florida Keys?!!

Me?!!

How much would you pay *them* for such a chance?

So I called up my cousin-in-law, Butch, to see if he could give me a ride. Since I didn't have a car at the time.

"Hey Butch, I got that job I was telling you about. Any chance you could give me a ride down there? I got gas money."

"Are you serious? That is so awesome! Don't even trip, cousin Truly. I have to work tomorrow morning at the truck lot, but I don't wanna see this opportunity to pass you by. So I will totally drive you down there *tonight* if you'll rent us a car. The bug is number seventeen by the way, and I can even get a cheap rental through our service department."

"What bug is seventeen, Butchy? That was kinda Out of Place amigo. You feelin' OK?"

"Oh I don't know. I don't have a Clue what I'm saying sometimes. Get all your gear together and we can be on the road by dark. You're buyin' all the coffee though, right?"

Butch is a big husky blond-haired guy with a bright broad salesman's grin. It goes along good with his always happy deep-set eyes. He reminds me of Butch Cassidy too, and I always tease him about it.

"Hey Butch, when are we gonna go steal us some fast horses? I heard there's a bunch of gold on the train up from Telluride. Come on Butchy, this workin' life is killin' me. Let's get the Wild Bunch back together..."

Butch is my cousin Fancy's husband, so her name is Fancy Majors now. Though of course it used to be Fancy Free, since Free is my Aunt Nancy's last name. My actual birth name is Truly Thomson, in case you were curious, but like I told you, I was adopted---after my parents got killed in a train wreck. So I ended up with my rather strange name, and totally by lucky chance. Strangely enough too, Butch's father was a treasure salvage diver. For a company called Osprey Salvage, back in the 1980's. So I guess treasure hunting runs in my family now that I think about it, or at least the good part of my family anyway. And I guess none of it is really that strange.

Since we do live in Florida.

I sure do know Butch is one good old boy, and I'm glad he's part of our family now. We need as many sane ones as we can get. You should see how cute my little niece is too.

I kissed my lady Dulce goodbye, and our dog named Pearl too. Then Butch and I drove all night. We made it down to Molasses Key around 4am the next day. Butch even helped me unload all my gear, then gave me a big hug and wished me luck. Then he turned right around and drove back up to Tarpon City for work. Like the true Road Dog he is. Eating up those miles, and doing what has to be done.

Captain Borders greeted me with puffy eyes, from hanging out with his friends too late the night before, at the library. He was wearing golden wire-rimmed glasses this time. Instead of the contact lenses he had on when we met. So he looked rather nerdy and bookish, compared to what one would typically think a famous rough-and-tumble treasure hunter might look like. Ole Jedd Borders is about five-foot-seven-inches tall, black very curly hair, super tan, kinda scruffy, only medium stocky, and is the most regular looking Jeans-and-a-T-shirt type of guy you ever wanna meet.

He reminds me of a high school soccer coach, or a community college science teacher, but the framed pictures of gold coins, treasure charts, and maps on most of the walls. Let me know I had come to the right place.

"Come on in Truly. Glad you could make it. I'm gonna catch a few more hours of sleep if you don't mind, but you can crash out here until we head to the yard. This is usually Wade's room, but he won't be back for awhile. Read up on the wrecks if you want to, or that bed right there is really comfortable too. I'll see you in a little while."

Jedd showed me to a room he said I could crash in. And if somehow you aren't already jealous out there. My fellow Indiana Jones® fans. I got to sleep in the company Map Room. With a seriously expensive Magnetometer laying right near the door. That room had a whole wall stuffed full of books. About nothing but shipwrecks and maritime archeology. I found out later, that the apartment we were in belonged to none other than the famous archaeologist Jefferson Benjamin IV. Who is also the company archaeologist for Green Sea Recovery.

I guess I'm really nothing but a big old Nerd myself, when it all comes down to it, because I fell asleep *and* woke up with a big old smile on my face. We slept those few more early morning hours, loaded some gear into Jedd's big dual-wheel diesel truck, stopped off at a little place for some coffee and a bagel sandwich, then headed on down to Dock Island. Where the boat was moored.

"So, Mister Free, did you look up anything about the wreck-site we been workin'? I know you got some college under your belt for all this stuff, and you said you're a strong diver. Did you look up about the Dead Sands? There's a lot of current running along out there where this wreck is layin'. You been eatin' your Wheaties®?"

"Yeah Jedd. I've been glued to the computer or a book about this wreck since you first told me about her. She's called *la Nuestra Señora de Santa Erzulie Dantor* and she went down in 1693. She was a *Nao* class vessel with 83 long guns aboard and seven on her rails. 457 passengers were aboard when she broke up over the reef, including 212 marines, *y el Marquis de Papa Relleno*. There were actually several members of the royal court aboard too, but only her young navigator and two very exhausted women survived in a life boat. To tell the horrid tale. The *Erzulie* also went down with an enormous amount of treasure aboard. The Marlin family first found her back in 1975 but even since then, she still gives up a pile every once in a while."

"Good job mister! All correct. What we do out here is dig holes though buddy. Burn diesel, and dig holes. We've been tying in all the new technologies to the whole thing too, so our maps are pretty sweet these days. Me and the guys have been putting coins on the boat, and finding some good artifacts too, but I know we are gonna come up on something good here soon. I can feel it. Here comes our turn, too."

We turned left at the next driveway, and drove in through a twenty-foot-high labyrinth of stacked wooden lobster traps before emerging into a big open space along a concrete sea-wall. Where marker floats of every color hung disorderly from bleached wooden racks, or lay in big color-coded piles, or were stuffed into barrels along the different lobster men's work sections. Waiting to be re-strung. I could tell the big stacks of traps were really blocking the wind too. Because the fine dust of the crushed-shell road hung hotly in the air for a while behind us after we passed. Then clung to the sweat pouring down my face. So it dripped an ivory mud down onto my neck. The Sun was suddenly way too hot and bright as we came into the more open area of the yard, where everybody parks.

The *Green Sea Daisy* herself is a converted 65' foot lobster boat, but now she has big aluminum blowers sticking up in the back, to distinguish her from the other boats. Like one of those caricatures of a hot-rod car with the big ridiculous exhaust pipes. Like in a Rat Fink® drawing, or that one Saturday morning race cartoon, with Huckleberry Hound® and Grape Ape® in it.

I wish I could tell you my first impression of the place was a little more magical, because this *is* a story about sunken treasure and pirates and other awesomely fantastical stuff, but what I'd really like to get across, is the seriously mundane nature of it all. How, right away, even something as cool as treasure hunting turned out to be just another kind of job. And when I first saw the place, what really kept me from floating away. Off into some fantasy land, dreaming of all the shiny stuff we might find. And what broke the magical spell of being aboard a ship...about to *actually* go search for sunken treasure, was: The smell.

Now listen, if you've never been to a South Florida lobster yard, but maybe you always wanted to, you could take this opportunity to conduct yourself a fun little science experiment. If you wanted to. In case you wanted to bring yourself closer to what I'm trying to say here. It's your book though. And we all choose our own level of involvement in these things. So, whatever.

Skip ahead if this kinda stuff bores you, but if you're in, here we go.

First, you want to go out and get yourself some cheap surplus animal parts. Any kind will do. Even road kill. They use old cow hides for lobster bait down there on Dock Island, but any kind of rotten meat will work. Then you want to put that yummy stuff into some kind of sealed barrel, and set it out in the Sun for awhile. At least a month or two. While that's cooking, you should go ahead and get yourself a whole bunch of dead shellfish, and some ripe rotten fish carcasses. You'll want to spread those all around out in your yard, so they can rot away and permeate the air with that unmistakable seaside aroma. Which will hopefully attract some stray cats, and we all know how feral felines can really perfume a place up too. If you are really lucky, at least one of the cats will die, so the smell of its carcass blends in nicely with all those other fragrances.

Then, on the first *really* hot day of Summer, when the scorched air is wavering on the roof-tops and those weird little water mirages are out on the pavement, from how hot it is, you can go outside and open the magic barrel. And take in a nice deep breath through your nose.

Mmmmmmmmm....tropical! You can almost hear the seagulls too.

Of course, if you want the real-deal Florida Keys Approved® version, you also need a few loose chickens running around, people hollering at one another in unintelligible Spanish, the taste of crushed oyster shell gritting between your teeth, and the kind of unrelenting humidity and sunshine that you only get that far South.

All those smelly thoughts faded for me though, as soon as I set foot on our vessel. I can't even begin to tell you how excited I was, as we geared up to leave the dock. Like I said though too, treasure hunting turned out to be a lot of work. And like I also said, it's actually *the* hardest job I ever had. No exaggeration required.

Treasure hunting is a dawn-to-dark work affair, and anyone who has ever lived or worked on a boat will tell you. Just being at sea itself is a constant unending every waking minute hands always full of something, putting every single thing back where they goes or fixing them, and making sure they stay dry and don't corrode away type of lifestyle. Then then when you add in Scuba diving, artifact care and categorization, *plus* underwater excavation, well let me tell you. When my head hit the pillow after the first full day, with the clear green water lapping at the hull outside my window, and the Sun's reflection still shimmering behind my eyelids from looking at it all day.

I don't even think I slept.

It was more like Becoming One with some big blue ball of light that I fell tumbling into. As soon as I closed my eyes. I stayed blissfully there until the Sun kissed the bottom of the cotton candy clouds. The next day. I woke up sore as Hell, but happier than I ever thought possible before. But hang on a second though y'all, I'm kinda getting ahead of myself. Again. Because I still have to introduce my good friend, and the toughest seaman I ever knew: Big Donny Hill.

Or actually, that's <u>First Mate</u> Donny Hill, to *you* landlubbers.

Donny is a fourth generation Conch®, and he used to play football for San Pedro State. He even got in a season for the Houston Patriots before tearing up his leg. He was also a professional body guard for the Tosh and Wailer families, down in Jamaica, and used to race big boats too.

Donny Hill is a top-notch seaman too. Him just being on board made me feel like we would definitely be making it back to shore. No matter what happened. We shook hands as he came aboard the first time, and I'm not exaggerating one bit when I say that his hands are so rough, and his arms are so built up from 20 years at sea, that I knew without a doubt. He could have totally ripped my arm off, right at the shoulder if he wanted to. So I smiled really big as we shook. But the easy fisherman's smile he gave me back, and his laid-back Deep Southern manners let me know right away, that he usually doesn't do that sort of thing. Not to people he knows anyway.

He looks like a sea giant too, and likes Hip Hop music way more than country, at least on shore, but we all listen to country out on the ocean. It's relaxing. Big Donny usually wears a Polo® shirt with the collar popped. And he's usually sporting a pair of matching pastel-plaid shorts, a thick gold chain or watch, and new white training shoes to go with the Miami Hot Boy® look he cultivates.

(And that's hot like a criminal, not like a model, in case you're not from around here.)

On land, Big D almost always shaves and looks freshly showered, at least in the morning, and his curly blond hair almost never looks messed up, except underwater. I'm not sure how he pulls it off really, because he works like a horse all day in the lobster yard, and we all sweat our butts off out there. His eyes are a really weird sea-green color too. Kind of like a six-foot-seven preppy marine iguana with muscles. Who you cannot beat in a staring contest. And he looks right at home on a boat. Like he was made for it.

He was my cabin-mate on board too, and his snores are bigger than he is. It's either a testament to how tired we all were at the end of the day, or just another example of what a person can get used to, but the sound of him sawing away at those big old logs in the bunk right below me, didn't even bother me. At least not after the first night.

Some people use a fan to fall asleep, or a TV on a white-noise channel, or some nice soothing music, or the gentle sound of lapping waves. None of those things work as good as the snores of a giant Lobster Man though. Maybe I just sub-consciously knew, that if there ever *was* a problem with the boat during the night, old Donny would know exactly what to do about it. So I guess knowing right where to find him made it easier to forget about how far away land was, or how strong the current is offshore. And about how shark-infested all the waters are around there. If we had to swim. At night.

But that's who I went to sea with for the first time. The famous Jedd Borders and the mighty Donny Hill.

Our other diver was named James Vinny. Kind of a tall thin gangly office-worker type. Who didn't really look like he belonged out there, but who definitely pulled his weight. James has a bald donut-ring hair-style, and a very timid self-preserving manner, but he definitely knows his way around a salvage boat. Truth is, I'll never be able to remember any of those fellows any other way, except: good, excellent, and heroic. Because those three guys showed me what I'd been looking for my whole life.

What I was born to do.

I'd worked out on another boat as a cook for awhile. A gambling boat that used to dock in downtown Tarpon City, at the pier. And of course I did a bunch of sailing in college. But I never was one of the people responsible for the actual maneuvering and upkeep of a large vessel before. Especially of a big old boat like the *Green Sea Daisy*. And as a actual paid treasure diver too!

Aunt Nancy always told me to go out in the world and find whatever made my heart sing, and my old thumper was just a-crooning away about then. Ya know?

As we motored away from Dock Island that first time across the wind-ruffled turquoise and purple-tinted waters. Out toward the real Florida Keys. The ones that no one can drive their car to---so are still worth visiting. I felt like a whole new world had just opened up for me.

The smell of the diesel exhaust playing on top of the rolling waves. The sunshine glistening on the pastel water as it splashed occasionally across the deck then ran out through the scupper holes. The rumble of the engines under my feet. The scream of the seagulls hovering right behind us. And the rainbow colored fish flying out away from the stern as we crashed through the oncoming rollers. All had me reeling dizzily in the pure uncut adventure of it all.

Life can be so amazing sometimes.

I could hardly believe it was actually *me* standing there. Alive and free, and exactly where I want to be.

We got out to the Matadoro Keys around sundown, and anchored in the lee of the main island. The Captain cooked us a very fine meal that evening, and he is quite the camp-stove chef I must admit. We ate and told jokes until we ran out of them, then turned in early to bed.

Around nine.

That was the first night I ever spent at sea, and I never want to forget the feeling of rocking dreamily in my window-level bunk. Floating just above the blue-green moon-kissed water rolling away to the glowing horizon. Nothing but a great big starry sky above us, and the lights of Havana just visible to the southwest. Snoozing away with my new friends above, below (ZZZZ!!!), and around me in the ship. All being rocked to sleep on the same blue waves. Like a pack of happy little treasure hunter babies.

I still love sleeping out on the ocean. More than any other place I can think of really. Especially in a storm. And I sure was glad I rested so deeply that first night, because the next day...we went to *work*.

I gotta' tell you.

Most of you wouldn't have made it through the first day.

We got up with the Sun painting a memory over the ocean. Then we checked the big diesel engines and got right into our morning routine while the Cuban Coffee brewed, and filled our noses with its dark nutty smell. Captain Borders shouted orders from the wheel house.

"Alright boys. Here we go. Free and Vinny. You two run forward and get that bow anchor up, while Donny gets the skiff ready to tow. We got a long day of digging ahead of us fellas. Let's all stay safe today and work together."

Sounds kinda simple and easy, right?

But a sixty-five-foot boat bouncing at her anchor in the open ocean puts a *huge* amount of force on the lines. So if you are in the wrong place at the wrong time, then you better hope It happens quick and clean. You better not get your hands in the winches or those big nasty cleats either. Or any other part of yourself between the boat and the skiff, as they bump together in the surf. Plus, any line paying out as the the anchor is dropped, can pull you over-board in a wet flash. If your legs get tangled in it. The fast moving line has a way of reaching out and grabbing at you too. So if you did the wrong thing, you could be jerked down below, ZOINK, like a tiny helpless minnow. Then you're under the boat, where those big eighteen-inch Brass propellers are spinning (chop chop chop). And it's a long slow way to the hospital from there.

The anchor clanked aboard safely, and the Captain turned us out to sea. Then he pushed the throttle up until the big engines rumbled. We ate some kind of breakfast while we motored out to the site, and the first diver suited up for a day at the underwater office. I was doing my best to stay out of the way, take it all in, pay extra close attention, and *not* jump up and down like an excited little kid. Because we hadn't even gotten started yet.

Now look, I'm sure maybe you've read, or seen descriptions of, how near-shore treasure salvage boats dig using the ship's propellers and engines. With three anchors, three winches, and our big metal prop-wash deflector tubes. Which are also known as mail-box blowers. But I'm going to go ahead and go through it again. For the newcomers. And also in the interest of describing a specialized type of archaeological dig. I also want to try and get across, that where *we* were digging, was even more challenging and dangerous than usual. They don't call it the Dead Sands for nothing, and more than a few seaman have met their grizzly fate on those particular waters.

So here we go, and feel free to take notes.

33

A modern day treasure salvage boat has those three big hydraulic winches I keep talking about. One on the bow, and one each on the starboard and port stern corners. Respectively. And those little babies are the real Stars of the Show. Because they let us move and hold our position, once we decide where to dig.

Captain Borders would pour over the charts and Digital Scatter Maps every evening, to try and decide where to dig in the morning. Then sleep on it, and be mostly decided by the time we got to the site the next day.

Our anchors were all eighty-pound Danforth style hooks. With twenty feet of two-inch chain. Big fat galvanized Steel swivel shackles. And those 200-foot-long two-inch-thick yellow floating anchor lines I was telling you about. Jedd would drive along until the GPS read the numbers he was looking for. Then he would give a silent forward wave out the window as a signal for us to let the bow-hook splash away. Then he would drift back from it. While accounting for the tide and wind, and looking at his map. Until he got where he wanted to dig.

Then came the *really* tricky part. Running the stern anchors out.

This was accomplished by tying a tag-line with a buoy on it, to the crown tripping-ring of the chosen hook. The anchor was then set up on the gunwale, by two of us, and we would throw the buoy-line out to Donny on the skiff. So he could tie that off to his stern cleat. Then Jedd would give the signal for him to take off. At speed. Which would jerk the anchor out into the water like a big deadly metal kite, and drag it along the bottom until the Captain liked its position. Then he would wave his arms for Donny to untie the line. And don't be thinking that we got all that right on the first time either.

Tricky!

The five-knot tide running against our big anchor lines created huge amounts of drag as they paid out. Which would pull the skiff off course as it towed. So it usually took at least two tries to get the anchor in the right place. Especially since Donny and Jedd were only communicating with hand signals over a distance of seventy yards, and they never really worked out a proper signal code.

Once the hook was where he wanted it, Donny would untie the line. Before a wave swamped the skiff. Then haul-butt around to the other side of the *Daisy* to repeat the above process.

And when I say haul-butt, I mean go *really* fast. He would give it the whole throttle and jump out---over---the waves. Then fly spraying up into the air like a Miami Vice® episode or something. Our tender-skiff was a little bitty fourteen-foot Glouchester® with a brand new 140HP four-stroke engine on it. And like I told you before, Donny used to race boats. So going fast on the water is just what Big D does best.

ZOOM!

Anyway, we would mess with the other anchor for another few minutes. To get that one set in place. Then Donny would race back to the big boat, and tie the skiff off up by the bow somewhere. So it rested along side us in the tide. Then he would join us back aboard. Usually too, just about the time the skiff was secured, someone would drop the dive ladder...SPLASH!...and our suited-up diver would crawl down onto it, to sit on the bottom steps. Until the top-side crew unhitched and lowered the big blower tubes down into the water. So he could swim under and pin them in place.

Once the pin was in place, the diver would swim out to the stern and un-clip the pulley line. Then swim back to the ladder and yell.

"Okay fellas! All clear!"

We would repeat the process for the other side too, of course. Then once both blowers were down and secured, it was time to move the boat into place.

Most modern treasure salvage vessels these days are equipped with a highly accurate differential GPS. The antennae for ours was mounted in the stern. Right dead mid-ships. On a tower off the gunwale, so that our GPS reading was right in the center of the hole we were digging. Of course the main readout was in the cockpit, but for our purposes the whole thing was also tied into a laptop running a Digital Mapping Program. Some proprietary thing based on Auto Quad® that Jedd had altered for his own purposes. His program has a blank white base map. Which is really just a digital Cartesian coordinate system set to read in decimal degrees...and thereby it served as a model for the latitude and longitude coordinate system of the Earth.

Got all that?

Go ahead and read it again if you need to. I will wait right here for you. It is a bit complex back there, but you'll enjoy the next parts better if you can really picture what we were doing. And you can probably find pictures of all that stuff on the internet too. So go ahead and use your digital tool-kit freely on all this as you read along, me hearties. We're in the future now.

So then, once all the digging gear was in place, and the anchors were all set. And the divers were suited up on the ladder. We would use the instruments and the winches to dial in our position, then get down to some digging!

I'll never forget sitting there on the dive ladder that first time. With the hum of the big engines behind us and the warm bubbling water all around. The hot tropical Sun beating down on us. The constant rocking of the boat beneath an ever-changing tropical sky. The smell of the Sea and the wafting black diesel fumes. It was awesome like I had never quite felt before. And I found out what all those other divers had *really* been coming down there for all those years.

The Freedom!

A rough circle about thirty foot across, and from two-to-six foot deep, full of sand, is no small amount of dirt either, kids. But you can do the math if you want to. Then go ahead and email the exact approximate volume to someone who cares. But all I know is, it usually took about ten or fifteen minutes of digging for us to get down to the bedrock.

Once he felt like we had moved enough sand, the Captain would draw back on the throttles, take the boat out of gear, and holler back: "Dive,

dive, dive!" Then whoever was on the ladder would splash away with a bright yellow Pulse-Induction metal detector wand in one hand, and the other hand on his mask, to keep it on his face. As he floated down quickly to see what we uncovered. And that's the thing about diving for sunken treasure, especially on a known shipwreck site. You really never know *what* you'll find down there.

Once the general area of a shipwreck is found, and you know where most of the major parts are, it's kind of like one of those children's plastic puzzles, where you turn over squares looking for the golden picture of a Treasure Chest. You'll find it eventually, if you just keep looking. So it wasn't even noon before we had unearthed (un-watered?) some very interesting artifacts. Lots of pieces of pottery, lead sheathing from the hull, and all manner of heavily encrusted objects. Upon whose former shipboard functions we could only speculate.

In fact, this particular wreck left Cuba only two days before she met her end, so she was *very* full of everything 495 people would need to cross an ocean for a month. Which meant this wreck site was just *loaded* with artifacts.

The noise of the engines came down a few tones, and as Vinny and I felt them come out of gear through the hull, we checked our Scuba equipment one last time.

We were also wearing metal detectors at our waist, so had to keep the wand-wire from getting all tangled with our gear as we got ready to dive. Which was actually a little easier than it might have been if we were wearing buoyancy compensator vests.

But real working salvage divers don't even wear those things. Because like I told you before, the current out in the Dead Sands will carry a diver away *really* fast, so the added drag and flotation of a BC vest would make it nearly impossible to stay in one spot and do any metal detecting, or hand-fanning.

For diving on the wreck of the *Santa Erzulie* we all wore: A full-body 7mm wet-suit. Which is plenty darn buoyant itself. A hard plastic back-pack to hold the tank on. A first-stage regulator with only a second-stage and a pressure gauge. No octopus. A really expensive Aqua Surge® pulse-induction metal detector. And anywhere from twenty-five to forty pounds of weight. Depending on the diver. Which all really meant, that when Captain Borders gave the order, and I let go of the dive ladder for the first time, the blue-tinted sand-dune covered bottom came up at me *really* quick.

James landed in the sand beside me, and we gave each other the OK signal. Then as we each gave ourselves a final check-over, we also tuned our metal detectors, before setting off to our assigned search area. Usually one diver works the middle of the hole, while the other one works the circular berm of sand and loose stones created by the prop wash. I stuck with Vinny for the first couple holes. Just to get the hang of things.

And in case you didn't know, I totally love being underwater.

I could probably take a nap under there if I wanted to. It just really does seem like I was naturally made to be a diver, and I have honestly been that way since I was a little kid. So I'm not even bragging. First kid in the pool, last one out, and my very favorite thing of all was fetching coins thrown into the deep end. So when the tide first started coming up, it really wasn't too bad for me.

I found out pretty quick that I could use my fins for lift, if they were positioned just right, and the bedrock that used to be under the sand was a big brown thirty-foot Swiss Cheese of crevices. Of all sizes. From ones you could fit your whole body into, all the way down to really jagged little small ones. It was all just eroded Limestone really, but it gave the bottom an underwater volcanic moonscape kind of look. All the little holes gave us something to get a hand-hold on to keep from being swept away too. Off into the not-so-murky depths.

However, by the time an hour passed into that first tide cycle, the current was quite a bit stronger. So much stronger that when we were hanging onto the bottom and working, the current would hold us out *perpendicular* to it. Like diving in a really fast river. So if we lost our grip down there in the hole, and didn't gain another handhold before we got to the edge of the hole, then there would be nothing for us to grab onto. Sometimes we did lose our grip too, and got pushed out of the hole, so we had to shove our hands as far down as we could into the sand and 'climb' back to the exposed bedrock. While kicking really hard. And if the current happened to be really strong that day, or something went wrong, you might not make it back. Of course for me, this is just about the level of fun I'm most comfortable with. Imminent threat of being Lost at Sea?

Heck yeah, let's go!

No one ever got swept away in all my time out there though. And I tell you what else, my new friends, that *Santa Erzulie* is a sweet old girl of a shipwreck too. Because for our simple bravery that first day, James Vinny and I were quickly rewarded. With some honest to goodness Sunken Treasure! Cha-ching!

James swam over to me, on our second dive, and showed me a round blackened disk about the size of an American fifty-cent piece. Which I knew from seeing pictures of before, to be an encrusted silver Spanish Coin! I bounced it in my hand for a moment to feel the considerable weight of it, while Vinny took out his regulator and grinned toothily at me. Then I gave it back to him without saying anything, and turned away to keep looking for my own.

We searched the hole for about fifteen or twenty minutes, finding all kinds of mundane everyday shipwreck artifacts like I mentioned above, as well as a few more coins. Then we worked our way back across the hole to the artifact collection bin. Which was really just a plastic milk crate with a dive-weight cable-tied into the bottom of it. Hung from a 35-foot-long rope down into the water.

We dropped our artifacts in as we found them, or if it was a coin, we would stick it in our rubber work glove, to keep from losing it. Then when we were finished searching each hole, we would climb back up the rope, against the current, to the safety of the dive ladder. Once we were back, the crew on board would pull the basket up, winch the boat into the next position, call up to the Captain to dig another hole, and he would mark it on the digital map.

"So how was that, Truly? We found some treasure! Old and Spanish too. So I bet your feelin' like a Real Pirate now huh? A true adventurer! We find those a lot out here though. Next I wanna find some gold!"

"That sure would be amazing, Jim, or maybe even some cannons! I never in my life, until a couple weeks ago, thought I would ever get to hold a real Spanish Coin. I keep thinking I should feel different now, but I feel completely normal. Like it's just another day at the office."

"Well that probably just means you belong out here man. Welcome to the crew! I know the snowflake is number six, but I wonder what's for lunch today. I'm already hungry."

"No doubt James! Me too! I get all Clue-less and Out of Place if I don't eat enough. Like an underwater grizzly bear. Rah!" Then several droning minutes went by after that. Each of us lost in his own dreams.

The engines revved down. The Captain barked. We dove again.

And yes. Of course I found my own coins after that. Nothing else will make your heart race quite so fast either. Just picture it. You're diving on a known wreck site, and the metal detector screams in your ear, right near where you just saw another guy pull out a coin. So you fan the sand and the current carries it away. Then another pass of the wand. A couple more sweeps of the hand. And there it is. Out pops a genuine Piece of Eight, and you're the first person to touch it in 300 years.

Notes:

Chapter 7 – A Pouch of Lucky Fame

I personally found ten Silver Coins on our first trip out, which I'm told was very good for a first time diver. So I kinda got spoiled right away. Though, to be honest with you, everyone finds good stuff when the Captain puts the boat over the right spot. As long as you can work a detector and use the dive gear, you will find treasure.

Our second time out though, I didn't even get to pick up one piece, because I used up all my Luck on the very first day.

I was really trying step up to the plate, topside. By running the winches, and helping to maneuver the boat. Which is the really important stuff on a boat. Anybody can dive, right? But those big winches are definitely intimidating, and *will* hurt you if you make a mistake. So during the first trip, only Donny and Jedd really did the winching. Because they had more experience with those big hydraulic monsters. Which is also why James and I picked up so many coins. They let us.

So then, on the first day of our second trip, I was trying to tie a line off to the cleat, while the winch was still running. Because you have to do it that way. You only turn off the winch after the line is tied, so you don't lose ground, or get the line jerked out of your hand. I guess we caught a wave under the stern at the wrongest moment, because the two-inch-thick line paying back out pulled my hand right into the foot-long galvanized cleat. Before I could do anything to stop it. I mean fast!

Luckily, Donny and Jedd were both right there next to me, coaching me along. By yelling different directions at me. At the same time. One in each ear. Jedd was on the left. "Don't pull it so hard! Keep your wraps closer together!"

And Donny was on the right. "Let the line ride loose in your hand Cuz! Or it can..."

ZYHOOP!

Too late. I was caught!

Jedd reached over and shut off the winch in time. Before I really got hurt. But my hand was very trapped in the cleat, and pinned there by the wet sticky line. They were both totally powerless to help me too. No one can move a line that taught without the winch's help. So it was all up to the sea. Either the line was going to tighten up again with the next wave, and crush my fingers *off*, or the boat would bob down into a trough and hopefully let my hand go.

Talk about being in a pinch, right?

Like I said before though, I must have cashed in all my Luck right there. For that whole trip. Or maybe the Treasure Gods decided to show me some mercy, and they let me off with a warning. Because the boat decided to bob down into the next trough, and it let my smarting fingers go. I hopped around a minute, shaking it off.

"Oh my gosh that was close! Oh thank you, thank you! Golly, you guys weren't kidding about that rope being sticky when your hands are wet. Wow! Those winches don't play!"

Then of course I made them both get away from me. So I could figure out how to do it on my own. Now that I had seen the danger. Then I ran both winches all day until I had it down-pat. And I'm sure I kissed my fingers a couple more times too, when nobody was looking. Because I sure was glad they were still attached.

Even though all *my* Luck was spent, our collective fortunes as a crew were on the rise. Or at least our fame anyway. Because after we had been out for a few days, and were feeling really good about working with each other, the boss came out for a visit. In his other boat.

James and I did most of the diving last trip, so this time out Jedd and Donny were making up for it. The Captain was down in the hole when the boss arrived. With his wife and a couple investors. It seemed like we just got the boss's boat tied up, when Jedd startled us. He burst the surface and spit his regulator out at the same time. Then let out a big loud, "It's Gooold!!!"

Like some old-time prospector yelling to his mules. Then he swam over to the dive ladder, climbed up to the gunwale, and carefully took off his glove. Then showed us a tiny little flake of 22kt Gold.

"This thing was under a mountain of sand! I kept digging and digging and it all kept falling in on me, but I sure didn't give up. The Spanish used to carry big sacks of gold dust on these ships too, so this stuff could be everywhere around us! The weirdest part is the little piece of paper I found, right next to it. It was like a little scrap of modern newspaper and it read: 'The star is number one.' I lost it somewhere getting back up here, but that was kinda out of place don't you think? Like the ocean was sending me clues or something. I know I sure felt like a #1 Star when I found this here flake though too! It's Goooold!!!"

"Hey, that's why he's the Captain! The first gold of the season! WOOOO!!!!", Donny belted so loud it made our ears ring.

Finding a tiny little flake like that, out in the middle of nothing, was certainly very captain-like of him. And Jedd Borders is actually a really great boss of the ship too. Very firm when he needs to be. Because discipline will save your life at sea, in case you didn't know. And he also shows true compassion for the people he works with, which makes people want to work even harder for him.

He's a one of a kind sea character too, that Ole' Jedd Borders. There were a few times at sea with him, when he would be doing something Captain-like. Maybe barking an order over to the skiff, or handling the boat in a funky situation *while* directing everyone else's actions. And I would catch a weird glimpse of how easily he would fit into some old black-and-white sea movie. With the ship in a big raging storm on the high seas, and giant gray waves as big as the masts bashing against the hull, and him holding on at the wheel while shouting orders over the howling wind. Like a modern-day Black Sam Bellamy or something.

That old boy will get you to work harder than you ever have before too, and maybe even yell at you a few times during the day. But then that evening he'll cook up a really fine supper, and bring it right over to you at the table. Like he really cares about his sea-dogs. And all that hard work pays off quick too, because the day Hardly came out to visit, turned out to be even *more* lucky.

Vinny and Donny were down in the hole around lunch time, and it seemed like we just got everybody a sandwich, or a drink. Nobody had even taken a bite when James popped his head up over the gunwale by the dive ladder. He hollered, "Hey you guys, check this out!"

He was holding his hand out flat, with something black in it. At first, I swear, it looked like he was holding out a little pile of pet-poop. Or something like it. But as he passed his find around for the crowd's inspection, people started saying, "It's a clump of coins! Oh, my gosh it's Treasure!"

"That thing was way down in a pocket of sand, but the detector just kept *screaming*...so I just kept digging and digging. How many do you think are there?"

It was kind of hard to hear James talk though, because Hardly Farmer brought like five other people with him, including a couple of the investors' wives. This was a fairly significant find too, so the back deck was suddenly really noisy and excited.

When the artifact finally got around to me, I could see there were what looked to be thirty or more Silver Coins. All encrusted together in a not-so-neat-stack. Which meant something held them together in this position until they corroded. Then *that* something had rotted away in the salt water. We all started theorizing about this new idea, and someone else brought up the idea that it was probably some passenger's coin purse. And the leather pouch held the coins like that. In a clump. Long enough for the Silver to oxidize. But the leather was now long disintegrated, and left the clump of coins in the same position. For three long centuries.

This idea struck me deeply as I passed the clump back to the others, because it implied someone could have been wearing those coins at their waist, when he or she drowned out there. Certainly I already knew that 492 people died on the wreck of the *Santa Erzulie*. So we *were* diving in an underwater graveyard, but to actually touch something, that someone may have had on them as they died, was very spooky.

After the coins were cleaned and separated in the lab over the next few weeks, it turned out there was one particularly old coin from the early 1500's in the middle of the clump. It was protected from salt-corrosion by the outer ones. This meant that James brought up one of the oldest coins found yet, on that entire fleet of wrecks, and in very good condition too. Yeah Jim!

We finished up the trip, and I know we found a few more coins and plenty of other artifacts, but nothing else big.

Not like James Vinny's famously rare Poop of the Realm.

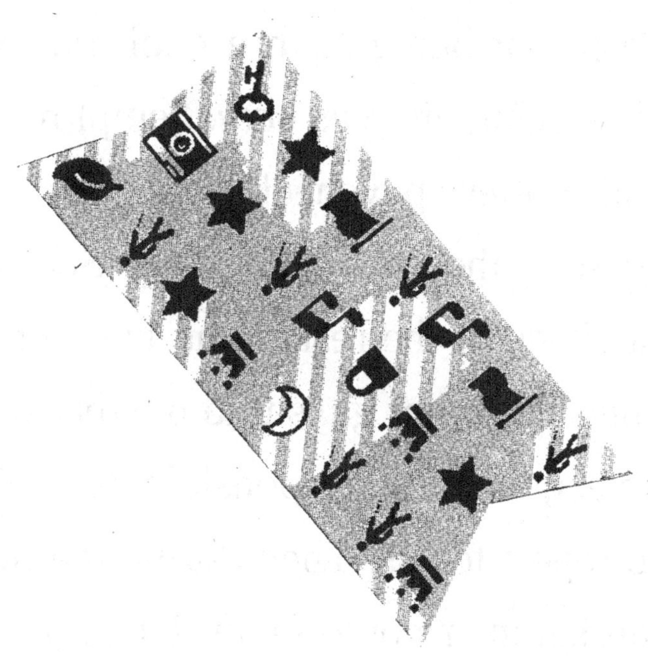

And that's actually one of last times I saw James Vinny.

Maybe one time after that. Down on Legba Street hanging out with the crew. But the next time *Daisy* left the dock, he was not aboard.

Captain Jedd said he had some big argument with Hardly, about money. Something about the drama mask being number nine, and Vinny wanting a decent place to stay now that he found some major treasure. Somewhere to live *besides* the couch in the office shack. Out there in the lobster yard. Which also meant he would need a significant raise, because a one bedroom apartment in Molasses Key would cost him his whole present paycheck. Which would be fine as long as he stopped eating or driving his car. But he must not have presented his case tactfully enough, because the boss told him, "Get Out of my Place if you don't like it, son! You don't have a Clue!"

And, WOOPS, he was gone!

There's actually a huge 'employee' turnover rate in the treasure salvage business, despite it being such a cool job. It mostly has to do with none of the divers being hired as *actual* employees of a company.

I know my hand-written paycheck said 'For Consulting' on the comments line. And sure, they took down my Social Security Number when I got that first check in the restaurant, but I never did fill out any kind of tax documents. The other guys told me that we would get a 1099 at the end of the year, and be responsible for whatever wages the company decided to report for us. Then during the off-season, everyone who stuck around all summer could claim Unemployment to tide them over. As long as the company turned in the right (false) numbers for you.

Standard Florida business practice really. Total irresponsibility on all fronts. If you don't actually make someone an employee, then you don't have to follow Employment Law. And how neat and tidy is that?

No Workman's Comp insurance, no health benefits, no messy paper trail. Just fold up the card table and run off back to the swamp, when the T-man comes around. I personally have been dealing with those type of Central Florida Rednecks® since I first started working construction twenty years ago. So I probably wouldn't know what to do if a Florida business-person *did* treat their people right. Or if the so-called authorities actually enforced the law either.

That would just seem weird to me.

It felt really good to get off the land again though, and I wish I could say I missed old James Vinny, but when it comes right down to it I'm nothing but a fickle little monkey myself. Just like everybody else. Truth is, I really only like what I like, and not much more. And all James's silly complaining got him replaced.

But the summer time calm was still in full swing though. High season for hunting shipwreck treasure. So the boat had to sail, and we had to keep searching. A call was put out to some other divers next. Who were working on a boat up in Port Fierce, and they hurried-on-down for a chance to dive. On the famous *Santa Erzulie*.

James's replacements (plural) were none other than Jack Valley and Pike Turner. And those guys are some way cool old-school treasure divers, no doubt.

Jack is a mid-forties retired investment banker. Who looks like he used to be a body builder too, or maybe just a racket-ball champion. He's got gray honest eyes, and always has something good to say. Pike is his main and boon treasure hunting partner, and is one of those laid-back country boys you find a lot of in Florida. With a calm disposition and dark serious features. He doesn't talk much either.

They'd been spending their summer so far, refurbishing one of Dale Marlin's old salvage boats. The *Miss Carolina*. So after many days of grinding fiberglass in a hot sweaty boat yard, they were very ready to get in the water. Like I said too. They were both old hands at the treasure game. As soon as they rolled into town, we got right back out to the site. Without much delay. Like everybody already knew their role. We all got to know each other better over the next few days at sea, and both Jack and Pike turned out to be some *very* interesting characters.

When they aren't doing stuff with shipwrecks in Florida, they also work on treasure mysteries inland, and were at the time looking for a big cache of British Gold.

"Yeah, we think it's hidden in a mountain. Out there in Kansas. The Indians attacked, so the Red Coats buried a couple wagon loads of gold before they all died. We've been talking to the land owner, and he says the flag is number twelve, which is a pretty big Clue really, so we're about to head Out to his Place this fall. After season is over. I think we're getting close too."

That was mostly Jack's project I think, and I'm not sure if he had to do anything else for income when *he* wasn't treasure hunting, but Pike Turner makes and sells his own really sweet fishing reels on the side. Which you should probably run right out and get one of actually. Because if he put any of his Fishing Luck® into one of those things, you will catch a whole bunch of fish with it.

Pike even brought a couple of his fishing poles with him aboard the *Daisy*. And I swear, every time I saw that old boy cast out a line...SHABLAM!...he would reel in a fish. It was like watching a fishing TV show or something, or like he had a secret helper down there underwater. Putting fish on his hook.

Both of those guys were really easy going, and never seemed to let anything get to them. They had tons of stories about treasure hunting, and they knew a lot about the industry. Super-strong on the boat and in the water too, because they had sailed under some of the best Captains up in central Florida. Working the 1733 fleet, out of Port Fierce. And for lots of years too.

One night, after we had been back out to sea a few days, we were sitting around on the deck talking and joking after dinner. When I noticed something glowing, and floating along in the water. Out of the corner of my eye. The other fellows noticed it about the same time, and someone said, "Jellyfish!" Just as the ocean all around us was suddenly and very well lighted. By a really wide cloud of phosphorescent sea jellies, that had just floated up out of nowhere.

It was like a huge glowing field of green lit up star-birds swimming slowly along all around us. The ocean glowed an eerie Jade color from their light. There were so many jellyfish spread around us, that we could even see the glow reflected onto the hull of the ship below us. The Captain got up and turned the lights off too. So now we could see the neon-green glow reflected on each other's faces.

We all got quiet for a solid minute or more. Just listening to our theme music, and enjoying the magic of nature. Each of us surely reflecting on how very lucky we were. To be right there at that strange moment.

Then Pike, who I don't think said a word all through supper, brought us all hilariously back to reality.

"Hey guys...we're Aquanauts."

There's probably nothing quite like lots of laughter and good cheer to help a fellow sleep well at night. And we sure all fell on the floor with that one. So that night I slept like a clear blue stone too. Happier than I could remember since being a little kid.

But look out though, you!

If I was starting to sound too dreamy back there for you. Or like everything was getting too easy, and we could forget to pay attention--- all the time. Then wake me up! Because the next day was crazy!

The wind picked up a good clip after lunch. So that by mid-afternoon there was a two-or-three-foot chop on the sea. Which I know doesn't sound like much if you're on the beach, but the tide was running the same direction as the swell. And kind of sideways-diagonal to the boat, so things were getting *bumpy* again.

Nothing too major at all, and we had worked through almost the same conditions before, but the skiff was tied off at the bow, and kept getting banged against the hull in a way that might capsize it. If a wave hit us wrong. So the Captain told me to go forward, jump in it, and motor her around to the back. So we could moor her off the stern, out of the waves and wind.

I was really still honing my open water skiff-handling skills, and what Big D made look effortless every day, was actually a *lifetime* worth of ocean knowledge. I was being as careful as I could, but I was also trying not to be a sissy about it. So I was giving the little boat as much gas as I could, without screwing up. This brought me out and around to the stern fairly quick. I backed off the throttle just in time, and was right where I was supposed to be. But then *just* as I was about to go forward and get the painter-line, to throw over to Donny and Jedd on the back deck, a little extra-big wave sneaked around the stern and threw the nose of the skiff up! Which caught me off guard so much, that my hand shot forward to catch my fall...but I accidentally *grabbed the throttle!!!*

I already told you how the skiff was only fourteen feet long, but she had a 140 Horse Power engine on her. So when my clumsy hand shoved the gas handle forward, the engine revved up all at once, and that little boat did what *it* was born to do.

GO!

Another wave must have come underneath me at that same moment too, because I swear to Jesus. That little boat stood up straight as a telephone pole, and for a full two seconds. Time stood completely still for a sun-baked fractured moment, and I will never get that picture out of my head. Of the skiff about to flip over, and Big D's hands flying to the sides of his head in slow motion. Making the classic "Oh no!" face.

Luckily, I stood still too. It was like every other dangerous thing that had ever happened to me before, even since I was a little kid, had *finally* taught me not to react right away. Because otherwise I don't know how I would have made it. My other hand must have gone to the steering wheel automatically, because somehow, I hung on and *rode* that son-of-a-biscuit. Like a surf-baggy wearing long-haired cowboy, on a fiberglass bucking bronco. With spinning sharp propellers attached to it.

Yee haw!

It was honestly like I was glued to the deck or something. I don't know how I did it. I hung there frozen in that second of grace, and took advantage of it to calmly pull the throttle back. Just in time to keep the boat from flipping over backwards.

And that, my new favorite pirate friends, is the single most dangerous thing I have ever had happen to me. So far. And it happened just like

Donny Hill said it would. Really fast, all at once, and harder than you can even imagine. I ran forward and threw the bow-line over to the stern of the *Daisy*, where Jedd and Big Donny were still standing. Shaking their heads in shock and disbelief. Nobody said anything for a few seconds, so then it was *extra* loud when Jedd barked, "Boy...get your self back on this boat! Now!"

Which I gladly, and quickly, did.

The wind changed direction again. Later that afternoon. And the tide was running strong by then too, so it was starting to get even more hairy out there. As the day progressed. We kept digging anyway, because we generally kept working until it was just too much to handle, or it got dark. And everyone *wanted* to keep hunting too, because it sure beat going back to the anchorage and just sitting there. Not finding anything.

But like I was saying, the wind switched around. So it was coming from the two o' clock position now, which meant that someone had to go move the skiff again. Donny did it this time, and the skiff ended up tied off to the port side. Where it was safe from the new direction of the waves. We were digging another hole right then too, so the big Brass props were cranking away underneath us, and the ocean was boiling blue-brown bubbles all around the boat.

Now, I don't remember exactly *why* I had to go over to the skiff again. Probably to get the hand-held radio I left on board or something, but anyway, I was trying to cross back over to the *Daisy* after I got it. The skiff was bouncing up and down in the swell, *while* the boat was rolling too. So as I stood in the skiff, the side rail of the bigger boat was moving up and down in the swell. From just right in front of my chin, to way too high above or below me. So this meant that if I timed it wrong, I could be seriously hurt, especially if I got caught between the two boats banging together.

I'm sure I was feeling confident from what I just survived earlier, and we were working on something interesting back aboard too. Something I wanted to hurry back to. So I didn't wait long enough, and just went for it. But the rail was slick.

BLOOP!

I was in the water and drifting back towards the big nasty propellers before I could even think about it. But I got lucky again. And managed to grab a free line that was hanging at the back of the skiff. Right at the very end. Captain Jedd saw me fall in, so ran forward and revved the engines down, and took the *Daisy* out of gear. Then ran back to the side of the boat. In about three seconds, flat.

He peered over the rail down to where I was pulling myself aboard the skiff. Like a silly wet embarrassed cat. And he gave me a very angry look. I thought he was going to holler at me for messing up again too, but he just shook his head and held out two fingers.

"That's two really close-calls in one day, Mister! You need to go sit down until we're done today. I'm not gonna be the one to have to call your mama."

Big D was right behind him, and chimed in too: "He's right Cuz, you better watch yourself. You don't want to meet up with number three. Number three is the heart, and the heart is number three."

"Okay Donny. I'll take a Clue. Third time pays for all, and I almost got knocked Out of Place on that one."

I know you've heard how superstitious us sailors can be, and the truth is, the sea just makes us that way. By being such a dangerously-magical place all the time. Situations like I just described happen constantly out on the ocean. That crazy summer held plenty of other hair-raising tales I could tell you too. To really drive home how perilous of a job working at sea is, but I have to leave some stories for other people to tell.

Those guys *actually* made me sit out the rest of the day too. Because everything really does happen in threes. So I got our dinner thawed-out, and organized the coolers, while they finished up the digging and put all the gear away. They wouldn't let me touch a knife, or the gas stove for the whole rest of the evening either. And if it tells you anything else, about superstitious, but super-tough sailors. Donny Hill will not knowingly sail out of the harbor on a boat with bananas aboard. Because he thinks it's really bad Mojo. And don't even *think* about bringing a Cowrie shell up on the boat. He will freak out!

However, I personally believe it's bad luck...

...to be so superstitious.

An awesomely terrible day to be sure, but what I will always really remember, and replay over and over in my head, and for the rest of my life. Is the next day...next day...next day...next day...

(Hey guys, I think there's an echo in here.)

Chapter 10 – A Box of Secrets

I'm sure it started out like most of the other days out on the site. Check the engines, get something to eat, get the boat in place, drop the blowers, then get on down below to the underwater office. But that particular morning, the *Green Sea Daisy* just, did, not, want to stay anchored where the Captain planned for us to dig that day.

Three different times we dropped the bow anchor and winched slowly on the line. To try and get the big main hook to stick. But the tide and the wind and the waves, just did not seem to like that spot for us. So they kept dragging the boat a hundred yards or more to the South. Jedd eventually decided to quit fighting the ocean. So we could actually get some digging done that morning.

"Forget this silly anchor! Let's just dig right here fellas. Go ahead and let her go."

SPLASH!

We drifted back, then winched slowly until we had a nice firm bight. Then Jedd had us run out the stern anchors, drop the digging gear...and get back to work. We had been out a few days by then too, but up to that morning, the most interesting artifacts we found were a couple encrusted sword handles, and a bunch more silver coins (yawn).

Jack and Donny were the first divers in. Once we got all set up. And all morning they pulled up piece after piece of broken pottery, and lead sheeting from the hull of the ship. They were tired and bored by lunch, but old Jack at least got to find *one* cool thing to show for all his work that morning. A big piece of beautiful blue-on-blue *Majolica* pottery.

Which is what the rich royal passengers and the officers ate from. As opposed to the more crude and simple stuff the sailors and servants used. There was something about the 300 year old ocean-worn shard that was still very elegant and refined. Even after all those centuries in the sea.

"Oh man, I wonder who was the last person to hold *that* plate?", we all wondered in unison.

Pike and I were the next two divers, and we ate our lunches on the dive ladder as the Captain dug another hole to search. Between bites we were talking and joking. About our upcoming day's first dive, and how badly the day had started out. We were probably even teasing Big D and Jack, for how they had done on their dives. Because that's how us sea-men are. And you're not gonna believe me either, but I swear I asked Pike, "Man, I wonder if we'll ever actually *find* anything. Have you ever found anything big yet? I know you've been doing this a while."

Old Pike Turner got all serious looking, and nodded his head wisely, as he finished his last bite of turkey sandwich. The engines were revved down and taken out of gear...and as if right on cue...the Captain hollered back "Dive! Dive! Dive!"

Pike adjusted his gear a little better, and took a test breath out of his regulator. Then as he exhaled, he answered me in his Central Florida country-boy drawl, "Some people do this for years, Truly, and never find too much of anything. But it sure beats workin' in some office."

He stuck his mouthpiece back in place and splashed off into the still settling cloud of sand below us. I waited a second. To be sure he had moved from below the ladder. Then I pushed off the bottom rung and let myself drift down with the sand. Until I fell to rest in the soft bottom below. Pike had already taken off to go work the middle of the hole. Like we decided. So I adjusted my metal detector and started to work the bottom of the big circular pile of sand around the outside of the hole. Which is otherwise known as The Berm.

I had only been searching for about one full minute, when I found the most beautiful piece of coral I had ever seen. Shaped exactly like a little piece of Cauliflower. A coral Florette. I took a deep breath out of my bottle of air, let my body relax as much as it could, and thought to myself, *"This is awesome. Who cares if we never find anything. I'm getting paid to DIVE...in the Florida Keys!"*

And I swear, that was exactly what was going on in my head, as my metal detector screamed a big old whining noise. Right into my ear-piece. REEEEEE!!! I passed the sensor coil around where it just was until I pinpointed the target. Then I began hand-fanning the brown sugar sand away with my other hand. I was sure it would just be another piece of lead, or an aluminum can, or some other piece of trash. Or *maybe* another coin. But as I dug down a couple more inches into the sand, out popped a seriously ornate piece...

...of Ancient Golden Jewelry!!!

Everything got really quiet for a second. I could hear my heart beating really loudly too. Because all of my blood rushed right up into my head. All at once. I couldn't believe it. This was it. The real deal. Sunken Blubber-Lovin' Treasure!

Yes!!!!

The piece of jewelry I picked up out of the hole was a golden broach or amulet. With enameled blue insets of flowers and ribbons, and there was a setting for a stone in the middle too, but nothing there. It must have weighed almost two full *heavy* ounces, but was only an inch and a half long. At first I thought it was costume jewelry. Because it looked so new and fake. Like the gold was poured and painted just the day before. But as soon as I picked it up and felt the weight, I knew my life was never gonna be the same.

I swam over to Pike and showed it to him. Briefly. I was kind of rude about it too (sorry Pike), but only because I was really excited and in a hurry to go up top. To show the Captain. So I didn't really let my dive buddy check the artifact out for as long as I should have, and took off really fast for the boat. He didn't follow me up to the ladder either, but just went right back to searching.

Only now with a really hungry gleam in his eye.

I climbed up the rungs as fast as I could, but then just as I got to the top...I remembered to slow down a little...so I could play a joke on the fellas. Jack was the dive-tender that afternoon, so when he saw me come up, he naturally came over to check if there was a problem. As he approached, I looked at him all stupid and straight-faced, like nothing special was going on. Then held out my hand and asked him.

"Is this any good?"

Jack's eyes about bugged out of his head as he saw what I was holding. And all he could manage was, "Oh my god!"

The Captain was taking a nap on one of the line boxes. Over on the other side of the boat. When he heard the commotion, he glanced over with one eye peeping out from under his hat. Then when he saw that high-karat gold gleaming in the tropical sun. It was like he went from laying in the shade digesting lunch, to jumping up and down laughing and hooting, like an old prospector, right in front of me. All in a flashy instant.

"That's gold fellas! Real *Santa Erzulie* gold! Well, what are you waiting for Mister? Get on back down there and get the rest of it!"

I didn't see Pike as I went back down to search. The tide was slacking off for the afternoon, but the visibility wasn't all that great yet. And I'm sure I felt like passing out underwater from all the adrenaline and bewilderment. Because that wasn't no little treasure I just found. That's the type of jewelry a person could buy a house with really. And you know I could barely believe it had even just happened.

I went back to searching the berm from where I left off before. Right under the dive ladder. Then I worked my way clockwise around the big thirty-foot-diameter sand crater, and I had made it around to about the two o' clock position and still not seen Pike. So I honestly have no idea what I was thinking about just then...but then the next thing happened.

And it was one of the most perfect and dramatic Movie Moments® of my entire, decidedly adventure-filled, life. I could not have dreamed this up if I tried. There up ahead of me and stuck about halfway into the berm, so it was halfway covered in sand, was what I could tell right away to be a small oval-shaped Lead Box. With the lid still on it.

The current was blowing the sand away from it in little sandy streamers. So it made the whole scene look like something out of an underwater desert movie. All I could think (and say into my regulator) was *"Oh man, I wonder what's inside* that *thing..."*

I picked up the little dented Lead Box and checked it out. There were some kind of dead crustacean hulls on each end of the lid holding it in place. Like perfect little natural latches. I knew better than to damage the box though. Even though my evil black-handled dive-knife was just *itching* to get at that lid. So I swam back up to the ladder again. To drop off my newer and better, but obviously delicate, treasure. Before I went searching for more.

As soon as I got my ears above the surface I could hear the guys on the deck screaming and whooping. They saw me pop up too, so they came over to see what I had. Of course they paused a moment. At the obvious mystery of The Box, but then started hollering again.

"Truly, have you seen this yet?! These gold chains!? WOOOO!!!!!!"

Donny took The Box from me and over to the artifact table. Where he picked up some other stuff, that I never thought I would get to see in my entire life. Much less be part of finding. Two or three huge Gold Chains. A gold finger-bar about ten inches long. Six or eight really ornate gold buttons with empty stone-settings. Plus two more medallions just as beautiful as the one I pulled up. And a whole bunch of little circular pieces of gold. With a rim on one side, and two little 'teeth' on the other face. Which were obviously for setting those missing stones. Into the other pieces.

So *that's* where Pike had been hiding.

"WOOOOO!!!!! Yeah!!! Treasure!!!"

We all took turns yelling. And sometimes yelled together.

"Can you guys even believe this!? Holy cow cookies fellas, we're rich! Oh my gosh, what a lucky lucky day!"

In fact, if you wanted to. Right now. You could go ahead and let out a big celebration yell of your own. If you're brave enough. Don't be shy. Go ahead and join in the fun. Because a day like that don't come around too often. So go ahead. Let out a big old treasure hunter war-whoop with me and the boys. We won't mind, and you know you want to.

WOOOOO!!!!

Treasure!!!!

Pike came back to the surface about that time with even more pieces of gold chain and another little gold setting. He looked over and chuckled through his teeth at me, because of how good he got me back. For not letting him handle the first piece I found. Then when he saw the mysterious gray box, his demeanor changed. To way more of a wary expression. Like: *"Hmmmm...maybe I better keep an eye on this guy."*

Because even though we were all on the same team, you know damn well we were keeping score. It's just what guys do.

I couldn't believe it though, a *big* old pile of that Shiny Buttery Ancient Stuff, and I'm not even going to try and put how I was feeling into words. Because that's the thing. There *is* no other experience like finding a bunch of sunken treasure. It's unique and special beyond all words. The artifacts we got to bring up that day were like nothing I could have ever imagined us finding. Though I know told you before. How I just *knew* we were going to find something good. Even that serious old man Pike Turner kept saying:

"Man, I had a *feeling* we were going to find something when we came down. My horoscope this morning even said, 'The diamond is number twenty-two', so I just knew it was gonna be a good treasure day. Yeah! Good old number 22!"

Man that would be cool to find some diamonds on a shipwreck, right? But they might be kinda out of place there. Since there weren't a lot of Spanish diamond mines. Don't listen to me though. I don't have a clue. I'm just another diver.

Donny and the crew moved the boat about fifteen feet to the stern, and the Captain went forward to blow a little more sand off the bedrock with the engines. So we could see if there was any more shiny stuff laying around. The engines rumbled and the sandy water came bubbling back up around our flippered feet. Down there on the bottom rung. While we talked, and joked, and hollered some more, and waited to dive again. Soon enough Jedd backed the engines off and took her out of gear. But before he could order us to do anything...SPLASH!

Away we went.

This time the search was much more meticulous, and the digging we just did with the props exposed even more of the very craggy bedrock. It also made the hole about ten feet wider in the back. And all those little holes were big enough to hide a whole bunch more treasure in, so they all had to be checked again. Thoroughly.

I signaled to Pike, that since he liked the middle so much, he could be in charge of *those* now too. The little tedious holes. Ha ha. And how I got that much information across to him with just hand signals, is its own little mystery really, but he understood perfectly. So I moved off to check the newly exposed parts of the berm.

And this is where things got *really* weird.

I was cruising along with the metal detector. Just doing my thing. When it screamed at me again, and almost made my heart jump into my throat. I fanned away the sand where I just passed the coil, and immediately saw a heavily encrusted metal object. About eight inches long. Which I picked up and set beside me in the sand. Then continued detecting. Because as any good metal-detectorist knows:

You *always* re-check the hole.

Sure enough, the machine said there was something else under the sand, so I dug it out too. It was another encrusted object. Almost perfectly like the first one, but a little bigger. And the second object was a little more immediately recognizable.

It was a pair of 300-year-old scissors.

I picked both pairs of them up, and was just about to turn around and head back to the artifact basket. When I swear. The water got a lot colder all of a sudden. I had a serious case of Chicken Skin® under my wet-suit too. And I promise, I even felt the scissors get heavier in my hand, and I was suddenly *very* sure that I was not alone. And Pike was way on the other side of the hole. Under the boat.

Right before my very eyes a two-foot-high sand-swirl appeared in the hole. Right where I just dug the scissors up. It was like a miniature dust-devil you see out on the plains or in the desert, but it was happening underwater. It hung there spinning in place, for what seemed like at least five seconds, before drifting up out of the hole and collapsing against the top of the berm. All the sand that the little mini-cyclone had been carrying blew away in the current, and out over the back of the berm.

But the weird part was...there *WAS* no current. Especially back there in the lee of the berm. And the tide was nearly full-slack by then too, so how could there have even *been* a sand swirl?

I let myself float upwards in the water column a bit, so I could see out over the top of the berm. Outside the hole, a dark turquoise desert scene lay silent and empty in all directions. Except for one stripe of extra bright sunlight. Playing and dancing along the sandy bottom as it moved away from me. Into the murky distance. Until it finally passed over another underwater dune, so I couldn't see it anymore.

I exhaled all my air, so I sank back down into the hole. To pick up the detector wand I left laying on the bottom. Then I lingered there for a moment longer, hoping my watery-visitor might come show itself again, but the goose pimples were gone and the water had returned to its regular temperature. And I know I should have probably been really freaked-out or something. I mean, I was ninety-something-percent sure I had just seen an actual Underwater Ghost®. So I probably should have been kicking and screaming toward the surface. But you'll just have to believe me when I say: Once you've been to some of the places I have, and seen some of the crazy stuff I've seen, even meeting a ghost underwater is kinda no big deal.

Shoot, we just found several million dollars worth of Sunken Treasure, so why *not* underwater spirits, too? But I sure didn't tell any of the other fellas about it though. They already thought I was crazy enough. Shhhhh.

As I swam back to the boat, it occurred to me that those scissors had probably been very expensive items back in the 17th century. Since they were obviously a matched set. And this *was* a shipwreck that 400-plus people died on. In sheer terror. So there was also a high probability, that whoever *had* owned those scissors, had also probably drowned while clutching them tightly. So I was more than happy to hand them off to the fellas at the top of the dive ladder. Just to get them out of my hands.

Spooky!

You can be sure we searched our heads off until the sun went down, but we didn't find anything else of note that day. The Captain had to put on the deck-lights as we headed back to our anchorage inside the reef. The sun was going down along the horizon now, and the lights of Havana were just becoming visible to the south of us. The anchor splashed away as the sun disappeared for the night, and we finished getting all our gear secure and ready for the next day. As the Captain got the steaks ready to go on the grill. Because what *else* do you eat for supper when you find Spanish Gold? Except thick juicy steaks!

You've never *seen* guys eat so heartily either. And every few minutes or so between bites. One of us would let out a huge excited "WOOOOOOOOOO!!!!" But of course try to time it right. So as not to make the other fellas choke on their food.

But it was endlessly amusing to us that we were such lucky lucky bastards. Who woulda' thunk it?

After supper we motored closer to Matadoro Key in the skiff. To call the boss and tell him the big news. Because there was no phone-service out by the reef. We could all hear him screaming on the other end of the phone as Jedd held it away from his ear. So we whooped back for him. Even though we were all getting a little hoarse by then.

We all said 'Goodnight' to the boss (in chorus), after Jedd told him all the details. Then motored back to the *Daisy* to hit the rack. So we could get back out to the site extra early the next day.

Right as I was falling asleep though, Donny let out another big "WHOOOOOOOO!", right below me and really loud. So it almost made me fall out of my bunk when I startled back awake. But then he started snoring immediately after, like he had done it in his sleep. So I didn't say anything, and just fell right to sleep myself. With *another* big old smile on my face.

Just like any of you would too.

Chapter 11 - The Chains of Pride

Most of us Treasure Hunters are a slightly jealous and very superstitious lot, even on a good day. I guess the other fellas figured Pike and I had scored enough glory for one trip, so the next day they kicked us out of The Pool. We were supposed to be running the deck that day while Jack and Donny did all the diving, and the Captain said he might get in after lunch.

"So don't even try it, you two."

He even pointed his finger and squinted his eyes at us, as he said it.

We anchored-up and started digging again. Right around the spot we were in the day before, and we'd dug quite a few holes by ten o' clock. The morning divers found a few more of those gold ornate button-looking things. And even a couple more gold setting-circles too, so we were all feeling pretty happy.

"Treasure in the morning boys! Did you guys ever think it would be like this? We're on top of the world right now! Nobody's seen this much treasure in awhile!"

The fever ran high. But since we got up extra early that morning, and got everything ready to go in the dark, everybody really didn't have time to do everything...that a body needs to do in the morning. If you know what I mean. Especially Donny, since he was the First Mate by then and ran the skiff, so he had to hurry and get it tied off to the stern. While I made coffee and Jack and Pike got the bow anchor up.

Then we hurried out and got all set up on the wreck, but I guess he hurried up and put on his dive gear too, instead of handling all his morning business. Because he was so excited to get in the water.

But there is one sure-fire physiological fact about Scuba Diving which no one can escape. If you eat food the night before, then drink coffee in the morning, and then scuba dive, you *will* have to use the bathroom. The kind you *don't* want to do in your wet-suit. Though I personally learned how to handle my #2 business underwater quite a while ago. In college. It's kind of a complicated process though, so maybe I'll explain it later.

And I'm sorry to be so crude and sophomoric again, in a story about pirates. Butt, check it out.

The Captain was up in his wheel house, going over the charts and checking out the radar. I think Pike was up on the bow taking a picture, and Jack and Donny were on the dive ladder. We were almost done digging the hole when Big D called out, "Hey Truly! Get in and dive this hole for me real quick. I've *got* to take a mean poop! My camera symbol is number two, and I'm feelin' all kinds of Outta' Place! Butt rockets in flight! Morning time delight!"

And yes. We definitely make jokes about this kinda stuff all the time.

It's a boat.

I should have had a Clue that something was going to happen when I got in the water. Because a couple dives before that, Jack brought up another piece of that pretty blue *Majolica* pottery. Just like we found right before we found the other treasure. I suited up as quick as I could, and got in without saying anything. Then when the Captain called back the dive-order, I really had to hurry to the bottom after Jack, to keep up with him. Because that old boy was on a *mission*.

He was already working the hole when I got down there, and shoo-ed me away when I swam up to say hello. So I took off across the bedrock to search as far away from him as I could. I was just swimming along and kind of not taking anything too serious, because I was sure there was *no* way I'd be finding anything else. Not after all the luck I had the day before. But then. Like it wasn't even real or something. I caught a flash of gold out of the corner of my eye.

It was a two-or-three-inch long section of Gold Chain. Of a color even darker yellow than the stuff we found the day before. I laughed into my regulator and reached down to pick it up. It turned out that there was even *more* of the chain that I could not see. I fanned the sand and tugged at it, then fanned some more, and before long I could see that I had hold of a complete gold chain. That was still mostly buried and tangled up in the crags of the bedrock.

I was in total happy shock. My heart was pounding again and I was even shaking a little bit, but I kept right on digging. Trying to free the rest of it without damaging any of it. All I kept thinking was how pissed-off Donny was going to be when I took it up to the boat. I finished getting it untangled and it came free of the sand in one long smooth motion. It was five feet long. And exquisite!

Another perfect Movie Moment®. Just like something out of The Deep, or even Fantasy Island, and just for the record...that was *two*. You didn't think I was claiming to be a Real Pirate just because I found some coins did you? Don't forget too, that this is the short version of this book, and not the only time I was on a treasure crew. So if you ever saw the whole pile of treasure I've gotten to find in this lifetime, even just so far, then Pirate would be the only word you come up with.

I swam over to Jack and showed him what I found, and all he did was shake his head in disbelief. He held the chain adoringly for a few moments then handed it back. But the best part was when I got back up top and showed it to the crew.

Donny let out an ear-splitting "Holy hamsters! WOOOOOOOO!!!!!"

The Captain only gave me a squinty-eyed suspicious look, like *"Who is this guy?"*, then gazed silently at the new chain sparkling in the sunlight for a while. Before passing it to the others for a look-over.

"Boy, you are one lucky mother-cracker. Way to go." Pike laughed as he handed me a soda.

"I've never seen a link like that before.", said Captain Jedd. "This is some kind of rare flat link instead of the usual round one. Very valuable."

"WOOOOOOOOO!!! Yeah Truly!" from Donny.

I was just plain speechless and kinda felt weird about the whole thing too. Two very major pieces of Treasure in only two days. How was I ever going to top that? And for that matter, who in the Hell *was* I right then?

I got out of the water quickly, before something went wrong, and gave Donny back his spot. We kept searching for the entire rest of that day too. Until the sun was long gone. I think Donny and Jack both found some more of those little gold settings, and Capt. Borders got in later that afternoon, but didn't get to find anything. He wasn't too upset though, since the Captain gets a bigger take-home share of what we all find anyway. Just for running the boat and having a captain's license.

The radio was on fire all day too. With well-wishers calling us to give their congratulations. Because news travels *fast* out there on the water. The Marlin Family called and said they would be out to visit soon. One of the other salvage vessels, who was working another wreck from the 1693 fleet, *La Cucaracha*, radioed to give us a "how-do-you-like-that", and to invite us over for dinner that night on their boat. And of course the boss, Hardly A. Farmer, called us up a *few* times. To tell us he had mobilized his press team, and that Seriously Big Things® were now in the works.

Exciting stuff, to be sure. But for me, and I know for the other fellas on board the *Daisy* too, we all just wanted to see what else was down there. I didn't really *want* to go back to shore. Because I was already getting that nauseating sense of dread, from knowing that a whole bunch of undue and unnecessary attention was about to be paid my way.

Yuck.

I hate it when people make a big deal out of stuff I do, especially when I'm just doing what I like to do. Finding stuff underwater. Whatever though, if they wanted to treat us like Rock Stars I guess it would be alright. As long as we got to keep diving.

That evening, we got ready to go over to the other salvage boat for dinner. By *wearing* the gold chains. Like it was just some everyday thing we were doing. The Captain had the little gold finger-bar sticking up out of his shirt pocket, and kept saying, "It's my swizzle-stick!", and even stirred his drink a few times with it. I got to wear the flat-link chain I found. Big Donny picked out the big round-link one, that looked like he should wear it all the time anyway. While Pike and Jack wore the other two chains, and got to carry all the other priceless trinkets around and show them off. Like a couple of walking, talking, multi-million-dollar mini-museums.

You've never really dressed up for dinner until you wear something worth $100,000 or more. And all the crew, on both boats, who were all seasoned hands at the treasure game, kept saying that the flat-link chain I was wearing, was probably worth a quarter-million dollars or better. Because they had never seen one like it. On any of the wrecks. We brought along the Mysterious Box to show the other guys too. And everybody took turns holding it, shaking it a little, and wondering what was inside. Like a Christmas present from the sea.

Of course all of this wasn't only for Show-and-Tell and bragging rights, as I'm sure you know. We couldn't really leave all this stuff back on board our boat while we ate. Because we weren't the only pirates around on those waters, and word was already starting to spread. And that's the the other thing about sunken treasure. Once you pull it up out of the water, it's like spilling blood. You may not see any sharks coming yet, but they are on the way.

Many laughs were had, and of course we let the other divers have a turn wearing the Booty®. As we recounted all the stories of how we found it, at least a couple times over. We stuffed our faces and laughed until late in the evening, then eventually we had to hurry back to our vessel for bed...and that's when things got even crazier!

Most evenings after dinner, someone would pull out an encrusted artifact, or maybe a strange looking piece of pottery, out of our saltwater preservation boxes. And ponder out loud on what it used to be. Or we would all try to imagine who was the last person to touch it 300 years ago. We forgot to have our little Show-and-Tell that evening though, because we went out visiting, but as I passed by the boxes on the way to bed, I noticed an object I wanted to ask everyone about. Because I didn't remember it being put in the tank.

"Hey fellas, what is *this* thing?" I asked, as I fished out a black and gnarled piece of water-soaked wood with no artifact tag on it.

The Captain turned around at the bottom of the stairs and answered "Oh I put that in there, because that is actually a really old piece of wood, and we found it down below the sediment layer today. Over by the treasure hole. All this stuff (he waved his hand out over the water to indicate the Dead Sands) used to be an ancient primordial forest a few thousand years ago, and that piece of tree was preserved under the mud for a really long time. Until we dug it up today."

I got a really serious case of Chicken Skin just about then, and felt kinda dizzy as I put the little piece of wood back in its watery bed.

Deep old forests? Hidden treasures? Underwater ghosts?

And Spanish *guys* didn't usually carry scissors on a ship. Not two pairs of big ones like a seamstress or a hairdresser has, and not next to a bunch of flowery fancy buttons and jewelry. So that water-spirit I saw might as well have been wearing a frilly blue dress.

Things were suddenly very familiar feeling, and I had to steady myself as I walked down the hall to my bunk. I even shed an involuntary tear, as my breathing got heavier and my heart beat sped up to match. I could barely believe it. The Blue Lady...

She was real!

The bathymetric map of where we'd been digging even corresponded to the dream. It showed a long high ridge of bedrock that ran along to the East for awhile, then went down into a deeper part. Which is exactly where we found all the Shiny Treasure.

When I went to bed, I couldn't help hoping The Blue Lady would come visit me again. But I didn't really think it would be too likely. Because somehow I knew her business was done with me now, and she had accomplished her task. She showed me what I was born to do. My special gift. And that's the greatest treasure anyone can ever find. So I said a little thank you to her, out there in her underwater forest, alone.

I finally got to meet her.

And maybe you're wondering why I think the ghost I saw underwater had anything to do with us finding that stuff, but think about it: A ghost doesn't usually have too much effect on the physical plane. Unless it's some kind of pissed-off poltergeist. But what about underwater? We had honestly been trying to dig in a totally different spot that day, but the ship kept dragging us back to that one. And I *know* I saw the sand move by itself, after I found the scissors. So it seems probable enough to me, that a disembodied ancient spirit *could* affect the sandy bottom enough, to not let the anchor get a bite. And thereby drift back to where it wanted us...or maybe you don't believe in such things.

I know for sure that I had done The One Thing® that my whole existence had been pointing to for many years, and apparently I'd had some otherworldly assistance in getting there too.

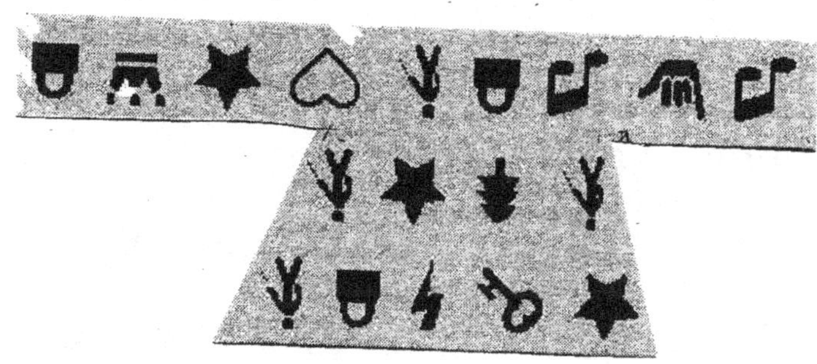

Then a few days later back on shore, it was finally time to see what was inside that box!

But the museum was much more of a zoo that day.

It had always been hot downstairs in the curation lab when we turned in artifacts, but *that* day was sweat-constantly-pouring-out-of-your-face unbearable. There were all the people I previously mentioned, plus a few more cameramen, reporters, and photographers, and at least twenty or thirty spectators, all stuffed together into that tiny hot little space, and all trying to be as close to the work bench as possible...so they could see.

Captain Borders was on the phone with a reporter from National Dublic Radio® to give a play-by-play verbal description of The Box being opened. Live and over the radio. Which of course was very cool, especially to an over-educated nerd like me.

Everyone else got even closer together, and the whole place got really quiet as the Chief Archaeologist and the Head Curator stepped up to the bench, to get the proverbial show on the road.

Both of those guys looked about how you would expect. With khaki shirts on to complete their Indiana Jonestown look, and one of them even had a Fedora on. Because you gotta look good for the cameras. They both had flower-print shorts and flip-flops on too, but the camera couldn't see those, under the counter.

They were using some sharp wooden dowels and a small electric power-drill tool to open the three-hundred-and-fifteen year old container, but I think they had done some of the work ahead of time, to make it go quicker. So the high-speed drill was really just laying out on the bench for show. The Archaeologist spoke very little as he worked the lid free. Then of course he paused...just as the box was ready to open all the way, surely to build the suspense a bit more, and of course to let all the cameras get ready for their big shot.

"Okay, here we go. And..."

As he pulled the lid away I tried to clear my mind of all expectations, so I could enjoy the Big Surprise with everyone else, and as the curator rinsed away some of the top sediment, with the freshwater bath he had prepared, everyone in a good line of sight seemed to draw in a sharp breath and exhale the same word, at exactly the same time. Like they had practiced it together beforehand.

"Pearls!"

That little five-and-a-half-inch-long box was completely *packed* with shiny gray pearls of all shapes and sizes!

There were what looked to be thousands of tiny seed-pearls, at least a couple thousand regular pea-sized pearls, ten or fifteen really large ones, and two other really big ones. Which were the biggest pearls I had ever seen. Even in books or on television. One of them was a long fat teardrop shaped pearl, about as big as an American quarter on the big end. While the other even larger one was bean-shaped, and almost as big around as an American fifty-cent piece!

Right as the box was fully opened though, one of the smart-aleck onlookers said, "Awww, it's just pearls.", like he was disappointed, or like that type of thing happened to him all the time. But then someone a little more intelligent replied, "Yeah, but think about how many *dives* it took to find all those things. That thing is rare."

That person was right! Just think about it.

How many dives does it take to come up with even *one* pearl?

Now, multiply that number, by the number of pearls in The Box, which turned out to be around 14,700 once they were all counted...and no matter what number you come up with...it's still a three hundred year old box full of dives. A link to so many peoples' pasts that I can *still* hardly fathom it all.

As I was allowing all this new and crazy stuff to sink in, I hung back from the crowd against one of the artifact tables. To the side of the room. And watched the rather bizarre scene take place around me. With all the treasure coins hanging from different peoples' necks on big expensive gold chains. Like the overly-proud talismans of some secret rich-boy society, and all the rusty corroded artifacts bubbling lightly in the electrolysis tanks all around us in the lab. It suddenly made me wonder how all this stuff ever seemed so important to me.

Like, what was I really even doing there? It's not like we were solving some great anthropological problem for anyone. Everybody knows the Spaniards raped the New World for treasure, and destroyed all the indigenous cultures with their religion, and that their boats tended to sink fairly often. And yes, it is still very funny to me how they never managed to figure out when hurricane season was. They just kept throwing more ships and people at it year after year, trying to keep the crown's coffers full. Greed versus nature, and nature wins again.

Way to go nature! Yeah!

I was reflecting too, on how all those crusty old things in the tanks used to be important parts of a ship, or maybe even personal possessions of people who were now dead for a long time. I wondered what they would think of all this. Us making such a big deal of it all, and profiting from their tragedy. As I watched the photographers and reporters plying their trade of making events and people seem more important than they really are, I was beginning to get really tickled at the whole scene, and had to keep myself from laughing out loud, lest I seem weird or rude.

"What a bunch of stupid monkeys we are. Like a bunch of silly little birds hopping around a piece of shiny tin-foil. Trying to decide who gets to put it in their nest. And the crown is number fourteen too, or maybe I don't have a Clue either. Boy, I sure do feel Out of Place sometimes."

The very idea that all this media-circus stuff was even happening, was very hilarious too. All just because of some ugly little metal box full of Oyster Puke®. It was the strangest form of amusement I could imagine, and not only was I about to catch a serious case of the giggles, but I was suddenly overcome by a real sense of connection to those ancient native divers. The people who first really found the pearls. All those hundreds of years ago. And how they too went out to sea and risked their *okole* to bring back Something Shiny. All just so someone else could be the benefactor of it's value.

I definitely understood those guys, and girls.

Every few minutes I would catch someone looking over at me, like they were talking about me, or like now they held me in some new kind of higher regard. All because I was the lucky bum who got to pick that crazy thing up off the bottom. Believe you me, I was in just as much of a state of shock and disbelief as anyone else. I mean, how would *you* feel, if you got to find an artifact like that?

The crowd began to break up after a while. Jedd and Hardly took off with the reporters for more interviews, while the scientists got back to work, and of course the speculation and comments continued as everyone moved toward their cars. I was hanging behind them all in the shade, and Donny was fielding questions as best he could. I probably shouldn't have left him to the sharks like that, but it was funny.

"What part of the world did all those pearls come from?"

"What is a collection like this actually worth?"

"Who did they belong to?"

Like I said, he was doing his best, but none of us had any answers like that yet. Finding out what was in The Mysterious Box only brought up a whole bunch more questions, and truth is, we may never know the real answers.

All the treasure we found was most likely personal contraband, because none of it was listed on the ship's manifest. The museum has a copy of said manifest from the archives in Seville, Spain, and they looked for it in the section concerning this wreck, but none of the items we found were there. This meant there *was* no person's name we could precisely attach to what we found, even though it all surely belonged to one of the upper-crust passengers of the ship.

And just to catch you up a little bit. In case you aren't familiar with these type of things. Every bit of treasure that boarded the Spanish treasure ships was subject to the King's Tax (*El Quince),* or one-fifth the value of the goods imported. However, anything that was worn, like chains or jewelry or clothing, was exempt from this tax. So the richer passengers would have all these really huge gold chains, and ridiculously gaudy gold-adorned outfits, that no one would ever really want to wear because they were too heavy, made to wear through customs. To avoid paying the tax.

It is also well documented that the minor-royals in His Majesty's court were the most prolific smugglers on the entire Spanish Main. Especially in the 17th century. But hey, everybody's gotta make a buck, right?

One thing we were certain of, is this: The little round gold settings and the corresponding gold ornate flat buttons we found, look exactly like the ones on ladies' dresses, in old paintings of Spanish royalty. There are several such pictures hanging in the museum, and *in* those pictures the gold buttons have Pearls set into them. Royals are not the kind of people who sew their own clothes either, so basically, we deduced, that at the time of the wreck, all the stuff we found...had probably been in the possession of someone's *tia*. Which is the Spanish word for 'aunt', but can also refer to a personal servant.

European noble-born children were always assigned a nanny/governess type-person. Who was in charge of their welfare and education, and who then stayed with them through adulthood. To function as a companion and hand-maiden, and thereby also as his or her tailor when required. Which is why the scissors were there with all the treasure. They belonged to someone's Auntie.

The Blue Lady, whatever her name was, had probably just started making a dress for her mistress on the very first night of the voyage. For it to be ready when the ship arrived in Spain two months later. Then a giant storm came along and took it all away. So her very last act on this Earth was surrendering her sewing kit to the sea, for me to find, three hundred and four years later.

Gracias Señora, y vaya con Dios mi amiga.

Nos vemos en la proxima vida.

Once again, it's hard to accurately describe the feelings that went along with all these events, especially after we put all that information together. I just don't know what else to compare them to. And I didn't really know how I was *supposed* to be feeling about it all either. Part of me wanted to become egotistical, and it would have been easy with the way people were talking to us like Rock Stars®. But I knew the inescapable truth about it all too. I hadn't really done *anything,* except go out diving with my friends.

All the real work was done for me. I was just like the guy who gets to pull the tape off at the end of a paint job, or a running back who catches a perfect pass in the end zone. I just made it *look* easy, and any moments I appeared to shine, were really just the Sun gleaming off the surface of a huge shiny pyramid, of other peoples' effort.

With a little help from some Friendly Spirits of course.

Oh yeah, and before I forget...one final clue:

If you scan the puzzle pieces onto card stock, instead of cutting them out, the whole thing is much easier to put together. And make sure to scan them all the same size too, or I guess you could just cut this book all up and use a glue stick to paste them to the inside cover. In order to solve the code. Since it is your book now after all, and that way no one can follow you to my Hidden Pirate Treasure.

Shhh...

Every ending is only another beginning,
and every seeking... brings <u>some</u> kind of finding.

Good luck.